Steve & Wessley in
THE SEA MONSTER

ISBN 978-0-545-61482-5

Copyright © 2014 by Jennifer E. Morris

All rights reserved. Published by Scholastic Inc.
SCHOLASTIC and associated logos are trademarks and/or registered trademarks of Scholastic Inc.

12 11 10 9 8 7 6 5 4 3   16 17 18 19/0

Printed in the U.S.A.   40
First printing, September 2014

Book design by Maria Mercado

For Leo and the Lake Whalom Sea Monster

Steve & Wessley in

THE SEA MONSTER

by J. E. Morris

SCHOLASTIC INC.

Steve and Wessley were walking
by the pond.

Steve and Wessley sat by the pond
and ate their lunch.